A BOY, A DOG and A FROG

by Mercer Mayer

To my family,
Marianna and Samantha

Copyright © 1967 by Mercer Mayer. All rights reserved.
Library of Congress Catalog Card Number: 67-22254
First Pied Piper Printing 1978
Printed in Hong Kong by South China Printing Co.
COBE
4 6 8 10 9 7 5 3
A Pied Piper Book is a registered trademark of Dial Books for Young Readers
A division of E. P. Dutton | A division of New American Library
® TM 1,163,686 and ® TM 1,054,312
A BOY, A DOG AND A FROG is published in a hardcover edition by
Dial Books for Young Readers, 2 Park Avenue, New York, New York 10016
ISBN 0-8037-0769-X

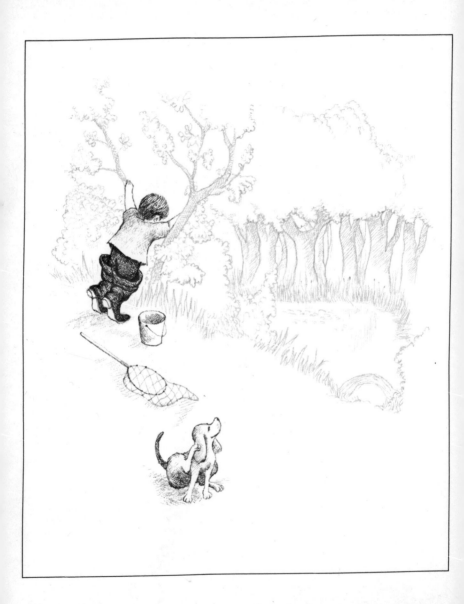